DEMCO

Alpha

Betti

Carlene Morton

Illustrations by Margeaux Lucas

Fort Atkinson, Wisconsin

Published by UpstartBooks
W5527 State Road 106
P.O. Box 800
Fort Atkinson, Wisconsin 53538-0800
1-800-448-4887

Text © 2007 by Carlene Morton
Illustrations © 2007 by Margeaux Lucas

The paper used in this publication meets the minimum requirements of
American National Standard for Information Science — Permanence of
Paper for Printed Library Material. ANSI/NISO Z39.48.

*To my family of listeners for their support: Danny,
Ricky, David, Casey, Gavyn, and Cooper.
Thank you to my friends, Gloria and Anita.*
—C. M.

To Mom and Dad, with all my love.
—M. L.

Betti straightened her tiara and bounced into the den. "I am Mighty Betti. I can slay evil dragons. No job is too hard for me!"

Betti's outburst startled Gravy and caused Mom to look up from her magazine. "I have a job for you," Mom said. "Go clean your messy room—it's no wonder you're late every morning."

Betti ran down the hall and into her room. She stared at
the clothes, shoes, toys, and books scattered on the floor.
Betti pulled on a pair of tights and one of her mom's shirts.
Mighty Betti can clean up this mighty big mess, she thought.

She crammed everything into her closet and closed the
doors. Betti called to Mom, "Come look."

Mom and Gravy peeked into Betti's room.
"Your room looks perfect!"

As Mom tucked Betti into bed she said, "I bet you'll get ready for school in record time tomorrow."

But the next morning Betti could not find her favorite jeans and butterfly shirt, so she wore her black jeans and rainbow shirt instead. She could not find her library book that was due or her Chess game to take for show and share.

Mom called, "Time to go."

Betti looked frantically for her book and game with no luck. Mom called again, "Hurry or we'll be late."

Betti grabbed a bagel and her bookbag and headed for the van, with Gravy leading the way.

In the media center that day, Ms. Bare said, "The library houses lots of information. You must know how to alphabetize to find what you need. Betti, keep your eyes on me." She thought Betti was not listening, but Betti heard every word.

Ms. Bare continued, "Being a master at ABC order helps you locate things more quickly. Today we'll use different centers to practice."

At the fiction center, Betti went on a scavenger hunt.
She read her assignment. "You are on a safari. You must
capture a book by Beverly Cleary." Betti pretended she was
in the jungle as she crept through the fiction shelves.

She remembered that fiction books were arranged in ABC order by the author's last name. There are a lot of books by Beverly Cleary, Betti thought. She chose *Ramona the Brave*.

At the encyclopedia center, Betti became a detective. She read the ransom note on the table. "I have booknapped Ms. Bare's favorite book. I am holding it in Nigeria. Find the continent where I am located and I will release the book." The note was signed "The Booknapper."

Betti tiptoed to the encyclopedias. The volume she needed was "N." She leafed through the "N" volume, reading the guide words at the top of each page. She found "Nigeria" in bold print along with a map, which told Betti that Nigeria is on the continent of Africa.

At the dictionary center, Betti turned into a spy. She examined the card labeled "Secret Mission." It read, "Your task is to crack a code that uses the word 'dishevel.' Write the definition. Hint: Use the unabridged dictionary."

Betti walked quietly to the reference section and stood at the big dictionary. This book has a gazillion pages, she thought. Finally, she found "dishevel." She took her silver pen and wrote: "to become disarranged and untidy."

Betti was proud of the button Ms. Bare pinned on her shirt. The words "Super ABC Hero" gave her an idea.

When she and Mom arrived home, Betti rushed to her room. She found her old Dracula cape and some magic markers. She decorated the cape with letters.

She dashed into the kitchen with her cape flapping behind her.

Mom chuckled. "And who are you today?"

Betti stood rigidly with her hands on her hips. "I am Alpha Betti, superhero, a master at ABC order."

"That explains the letters. What are you going to alphabetize?" Mom asked.

"My closet," replied Betti.

She raced into her room. "Alpha Betti can survive an avalanche," she declared. She yanked the closet door open and jumped aside. Shoes, books, and toys slid into the room. Alpha Betti stood atop the mound of items.

Alpha Betti can conquer this mountain, she thought.
She sorted everything into smaller heaps.

She pulled all of the clothes from the floor and
piled them onto a chair.

My first quest is the books, thought Alpha Betti. She put the books by the same author in separate stacks and decided to tackle the books by Andrew Clements. Which goes first? *The Jacket, The Landry News, The Janitor's Boy, Frindle,* or *A Week in the Woods*?

She remembered to ignore the words "a," "an," and "the" at the beginning when alphabetizing by title. Once she sorted Clements's books, she slid *Frindle* onto the bookshelf, followed by the other four. Betti put the rest of her books in ABC order lickety-split.

Next she moved on to her clothes and shoes. Alpha Betti set her shoes on the closet floor. Gravy helped.

She put her clothes on hangers. She asked herself, which goes first? Shirts, pants, skirts, dresses, or sweaters? She hung her dresses in the closet, then her pants. Oh my, thought Betti, there are three words that start with the same letter. She remembered to look at the second letter to finish the job—shirts, skirts, then sweaters. All done!

Alpha Betti stood by the pile of toys. She checked her watch; it was almost time for her to recharge her energy. I'll just organize my board games, she thought. Which goes first? Memory, Checkers, Chess, Trivia Junior, or Bingo? Uh-oh. Checkers and Chess have the same first three letters.

Betti remembered to keep looking until she saw a different letter. She stacked her games in order with Bingo on top and Trivia Junior on the bottom, then she slid the games into her cabinet.

The next morning, Alpha Betti was ready for school in record time. Wearing her favorite jeans and butterfly shirt, she brought her Chess game and library book into the kitchen.

"You're so speedy!" Mom said.

"It's easy to get ready with my closet in ABC order. I can help you put the kitchen in order. Where can I start—the spices, the pantry, the refrigerator?" Betti began to pull cans from the pantry.

"We better save that for later," Mom said.

Betti answered, "But you can find things fast
when you're a master at ABC order."

"You can alphabetize the kitchen after school.
Now let's get going," Mom replied with a smile.